W0384639

lighthouse BASIC 2

Grammarmaster

Deinen Grammarmaster findest du auch in der **Cornelsen Lernen App**.

Siehst du eines dieser Symbole in deinem Grammarmaster, findest du in der App …

- alle **Erklärfilme**
- **Lösungen** zu den Aufgaben

Cornelsen

BASIC
lighthouse 2

Grammarmaster

Im Auftrag des Verlages erarbeitet von
James Styring, Charlbury

In Zusammenarbeit mit der Englischredaktion
Klaus Unger (Projektleitung), Anja Zieschang

Beratende Mitwirkung
Daniel Henn, Frankfurt/Main; Christina Sieber, Schorndorf

Lizenzmanagement
Silke Kirchhoff

Illustrationen
Matthias Pflügner, Berlin
Irina Zinner, Hamburg

Fotos
Anja Poehlmann, Brighton
Für die freundliche Unterstützung danken wir der Varndean School, Brighton

Umschlaggestaltung
Rosendahl, Berlin

Layoutkonzept
Klein & Halm, Berlin

Layout und technische Umsetzung
PER MEDIEN & MARKETING GmbH, Braunschweig

Druck
AZ Druck und Datentechnik GmbH, Kempten

PEFC-zertifiziert
Dieses Produkt stammt aus nachhaltig bewirtschafteten Wäldern und kontrollierten Quellen
PEFC/04-31-2260
www.pefc.de

www.cornelsen.de

1. Auflage, 1. Druck 2024
978-3-06-034635-6

So lernst du mit Lighthouse U2

Impressum 2

Inhaltsverzeichnis 3

Hello again!
The last day of the holidays
REVISION: Das present progressive 4

Unit 1
Travel and holidays
Das simple past mit *be* 5
Das simple past: Bejahte Aussagesätze mit regelmäßigen Verben 6
Das simple past: Bejahte Aussagesätze mit unregelmäßigen Verben 7
Das simple past: Verneinte Aussagesätze 9

Unit 2
Friends and heroes
Das simple past: Fragen und Kurzantworten 12
Das simple past: Fragen mit Fragewörtern 14
Nebensätze mit Konjunktionen 15

Unit 3
Activities and games
Das Futur mit going to 17
Die Steigerung von Adjektiven: Komparativ 19
Die Steigerung von Adjektiven: Superlativ 21

Unit 4
Celebrate!
Some / any 36
A little / a few 38
Zusammensetzungen mit *some* und *any* 39
Das present perfect 40

Unit 5
Getting ready for the future
Das will-future: Bejahte und verneinte Aussagesätze 43
Das will-future: Fragen und Kurzantworten 45
Die Wortstellung 47

Auf einen Blick 51

Lösungen 23
Quellenverzeichnis U3

Hello again!
The last day of the holidays

Erklär-film

REVISION: Das present progressive

Mit dem *present progressive* sagst du, was jemand jetzt gerade tut. Du beschreibst damit auch, was auf Bildern passiert. Signalwörter für das *present progressive* sind: now (jetzt, gerade), at the moment (im Moment), today (heute).

Das *present progressive* besteht aus zwei Teilen:
be + *verb* + *-ing*
is *watching*

She's looking happy in the photo. (Sie sieht glücklich aus auf dem Foto.)

My parents aren't making lunch today. (Meine Eltern machen heute kein Mittagessen.)

What are you doing at the moment? (Was machst du gerade?)

be
I am / 'm not
he/she/it is / isn't
we/you/they are / aren't

► SB p. 173

1 REVISION A day on the beach

What are or aren't the people doing at the moment? Look at the picture and write sentences.
Was machen die Leute auf dem Bild gerade? Was machen sie nicht? Schreibe Sätze.

1 Sonya *is* ______ playing volleyball. She *isn't* ______ swimming.

2 Josh ______ standing on the beach. He ______ surfing.

3 Ben and his dad ______ building a sandcastle. They ______ having a picnic.

4 Justine and her friend ______ taking a photo. They ______ sleeping.

5 Holly's dog ______ eating. It ______ running for a ball.

► Check

Unit 1
Travel and holidays

Erklär-film

Das simple past mit *be*

Mit dem *simple past* sprichst du über Dinge, die in der Vergangenheit geschehen sind. Du verwendest es oft mit Zeitangaben wie yesterday (gestern), last week (letzte Woche), in 2022 (2022).

Das Verb *be* hat besondere *simple past*-Formen:

A **bejahte und verneinte Aussagesätze**

I / He / She / It / Noah / Mum	was / wasn't	at home.
You / We / They / My friends	were / weren't	at home.

B **Fragen**

	Was	he / she	at home?
	Were	you / they	at home?
Where	were	you	?

▶ SB p. 13, p. 174

1 How was your holiday?

Circle the right words. *Kreise die richtigen Wörter ein.*

Toby How was your holiday?

Lucy It was / were great, thanks. We was / were in Spain. Were you here in Brighton all the time?

Toby No, we wasn't / weren't. We was / were in Wales for two weeks. It was / were cold and windy. Was the weather good in Spain?

Lucy It was / were sunny every day. The weather was / were perfect!

2 The first day back at school

Look at the picture and complete the sentences with *was* or *were*.
Schau dir das Bild an und vervollständige die Sätze mit was *oder* were.

1 Was Noah's shirt blue? – No, it ____________ white.

2 Was Sunita's skirt black? – Yes, it ____________.

3 Were Noah and Zane's uniforms the same? – Yes, they ____________.

▶ Check

Erklär-
film

Das simple past: Bejahte Aussagesätze mit regelmäßigen Verben

Bei regelmäßigen Verben hängst du *-ed* an das Verb an. Es gibt nur eine Form für alle Personen:

I/you/he/she/it/we/you/they talked, looked, watched, …

Endet das Verb auf *-e*, hängst du nur *-d* an: *dance → danced, like → liked, save → saved*

► SB p. 14, p. 174

3 In the summer holidays

Circle the right word. *Kreise das richtige Wort ein.*

1 Tim played / wanted basketball most days.

2 Evie helped / travelled to Scotland with her dog.

3 Lily liked / cycled near her aunt's house in Poland.

4 Sunita and her family enjoyed / moved Prague.

5 Ravi listened / talked to a concert on Brighton Pier.

4 Lisa's holiday

Lisa is talking about her last holidays. Write the verbs in the simple past.
Lisa erzählt von ihren letzten Ferien. Schreibe die Verben im simple past.

My parents were at work, so I (1) stayed *(stay) in Brighton in the holidays. I (2) ______ (visit) my grandma for some days. She's nice. She lives in Hove. I often (3) ______ (cycle) to the beach. I (4) ______ (play) beach volleyball. Sometimes I (5) ______ (watch) a film at the cinema. One night I was at Ravi's birthday party. We (6) ______ (talk), (7) ______ (listen) to music and (8) ______ (dance). I (9) ______ (like) the Pride Parade too. There were 300,000 people in Brighton that day.*

► Check

Das simple past: Bejahte Aussagesätze mit unregelmäßigen Verben

Einige Verben haben unregelmäßige Formen im *simple past*, z. B.:

do	→	did	run	→	ran
go	→	went	see	→	saw
have	→	had	write	→	wrote

Diese Formen musst du lernen.

▸ SB p. 16, p. 174, p. 271

5 Irregular verbs

a) **Write the simple past forms. You can use your Student's book page 271 for help.** *Schreibe die simple past-Formen. Wenn du Hilfe brauchst, kannst du in deinem Schulbuch auf Seite 271 nachschauen.*

1 be	was / ______	5 make	______
2 buy	______	6 meet	______
3 eat	______	7 sit	______
4 hear	______	8 take	______

b) **Complete the sentences. Use simple past forms from the grammar box and from a).** *Vervollständige die Sätze. Verwende simple past-Formen aus dem Grammatikkasten sowie aus a).*

1 We *were* ______ (be) at the Pride Parade last summer.

2 I ______ (hear) a cool song on the radio yesterday.

3 She ______ (do) her homework in the school library last Friday.

4 He ______ (write) some messages on his phone this morning.

5 We ______ (buy) a present for you last week.

6 My dad ______ (run) a marathon in May.

7 Katie ______ (sit) at the table next to me yesterday.

8 Marcus and I ______ (meet) at 11.30 last Sunday.

▸ Check

6 Lily and Alice's holidays

Complete the sentences with the words from the boxes.
Vervollständige die Sätze mit den Wörtern aus den Kästen.

did • ~~flew~~ • had • took • visited • went

Lily and her mum (1) flew ____________ to Poland and (2) ____________ Lily's aunt and uncle. They (3) ____________ lots of different things. One day they (4) ____________ her aunt and uncle's bikes and (5) ____________ around Krakow. They (6) ____________ lots of fun.

cooked • loved • sang • took • was • went • were

Alice (7) ____________ to Wales with her dad and her brother. It was a long journey – it (8) ____________ eight hours! They (9) ____________ on a campsite. It (10) ____________ a bit cold, but they (11) ____________ it! In the evenings they (12) ____________ barbecues and they (13) ____________ songs by the fire.

7 What about you?

Write sentences about you. *Schreibe Sätze über dich.*

Ideas
to my grandma / mum / dad / best friend / ...
a film / concert / TV show / some dancers on the street / ...
basketball / football / a game with my sister / ...
pizza / ice cream / cake / spaghetti / ...

1 I talked ____________________________________ this morning.

2 I watched ____________________________________ last weekend.

3 I played ____________________________________ yesterday.

4 I ate ____________________________________ last week.

► Check

Erklär-film

Das simple past: Verneinte Aussagesätze

Willst du sagen, dass etwas nicht geschah, stellst du didn't vor die Grundform des Verbs. *Didn't* verwendest du bei allen Personen.

Ben didn't like the food. (Ben mochte das Essen nicht.)

We didn't go out last Friday. (Wir gingen letzten Freitag nicht aus.)

► SB p. 20, p. 175

8 Scout's summer (1)

a) **Write the infinitive of the blue verbs.** *Schreibe die Grundform der blauen Verben.*

b) **Write negative sentences.** *Schreibe verneinte Sätze.*

1

Scout ate fish and chips. eat

She didn't eat ______ burgers.

2

Scout flew over Brighton Pier. ______

She ______ over Blackpool Pier.

3

Scout danced in the rain. ______

She ______ in the sun.

4

Scout wore a tie. ______

She ______ a blazer.

5

Scout walked on the pier. ______

She ______ in the road.

6

Scout saw a lot of tourists. ______

She ______ Lily or Zane.

► Check

9 Some mistakes

Correct the mistakes. *Korrigiere die Fehler.*

1 We don't go to the football match last week. Was it good? *We didn't go* __________

2 Your teacher didn't gave you homework yesterday. __________

3 I didn't knows about the party on Saturday night. Who was there? __________

4 It doesn't rain last weekend. __________

10 Your last holidays

Write four positive or negative sentences about your last holidays. You can use the ideas in the pictures or your own ideas. *Schreibe vier bejahte oder verneinte Sätze über deine letzten Ferien. Nutze dazu die Ideen in den Bildern oder deine eigenen Ideen.*

flew / didn't fly | to Spain / Turkey / ...

bought / didn't buy | a present / some nice food / ice cream / ...

cooked / didn't cook | some nice food / a paella / every night with my family / ...

swam / didn't swim | in the sea / in a pool / ...

On my last holiday __________

____

____

____

▸ Check

11 Revision Scout's summer (2)

Write the correct forms of the verbs in the simple past. Blue verbs are regular, orange verbs are irregular. *Schreibe die richtigen Formen der Verben im simple past. Blaue Verben sind regelmäßige Verben, orangefarbene Verben sind unregelmäßige Verben.*

Scout wasn't away in the holidays. She (1) *was* (be) in Brighton all summer. She (2) ______________ (fly) around the city and she (3) ______________ (enjoy) the good weather. Scout (4) ______________ (relax) on the beach and she (5) ______________ (eat) a lot of food too. There (6) ______________ (be) lots of tourists and some of them (7) ______________ (give) their fish and chips to Scout!

12 Revision Reasons why

Write negative sentences in the simple past. *Schreibe verneinte Sätze im simple past.*

1 We *didn't go* (go) to the cinema last weekend because we *didn't have* (have) time.

2 Ravi ______________ (visit) us last weekend because he ______________ (get) our invitation.

3 I ______________ (finish) my pizza for lunch because I ______________ (be) hungry.

4 The students ______________ (be) in class yesterday because it ______________ (be) a school day.

5 I ______________ (see) the Loch Ness Monster in Scotland because I ______________ (go) to Loch Ness.

▸ Check

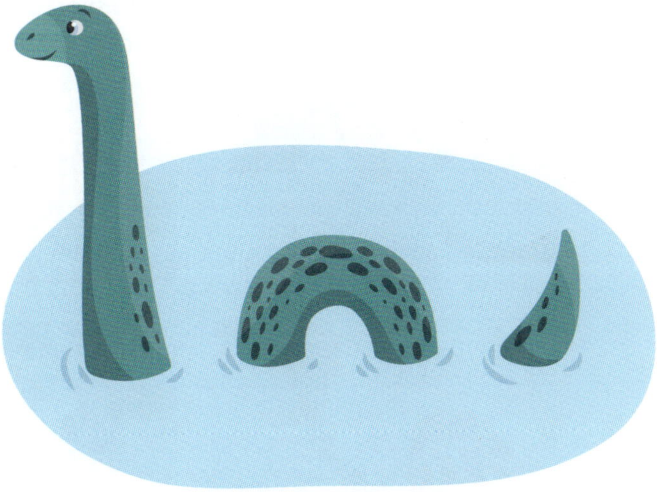

Unit 2
Friends and heroes

Erklär-film

Das simple past: Fragen und Kurzantworten

Fragen im *simple past* bildest du mit did und der Grundform des Verbs. Auf Entscheidungsfragen antwortest du mit Kurzantworten.

Did Gina visit her friends last week? – Yes, she did. / No, she didn't.
(Hat Gina letzte Woche ihre Freunde besucht? – Ja, hat sie. / Nein, hat sie nicht.)

► SB p. 46, p. 175

1 Yes, I did!

a) **Write questions.** *Schreibe Fragen.*

1 Did ______ she play football? Yes ______, she did ______.

2 ______ they walk to school? No ______, they didn't ______.

3 ______ he do the homework? ______, he ______.

4 ______ we go shopping? ______, we ______.

5 ______ you get the train? ______, I ______.

6 ______ she swim in the pool? ______, she ______.

b) **Look at the pictures from last week. Write short answers.**
Sieh dir die Bilder von letzter Woche an. Schreibe Kurzantworten.

1

2

3

4

5

6

► Check

2 The friends' holidays

   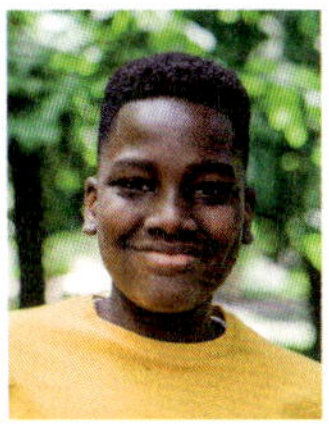

a) **Write questions with the verbs on the right.** *Schreibe Fragen mit den Verben rechts.*

visit · stay · go · travel · have

1 ________ Sunita's family ________ Prague?

2 ________ Sunita ________ on a campsite?

3 ________ Noah ________ on holiday to Wales?

4 ________ Lily ________ to Poland?

5 ________ Zane's apartment ________ a pool?

b) **Match the short answers with the questions from a).** *Ordne die Kurzantworten den Fragen aus a) zu.*

1 Yes, they did.	___ Yes, it did.	___ No, he didn't.	___ Yes, she did.	___ No, she didn't.

c) **Look at pages 12–13 in your Student's book and check your answers.** *Schau dir die Seiten 12–13 in deinem Schulbuch an und überprüfe die Antworten.*

3 Did you ...?

Write simple past questions. Answer the questions for you.
Schreibe Fragen im simple past. Beantworte die Fragen für dich.

1 you / do / Did / sport last weekend?
Did you do sport last weekend? – Yes, I did.

2 you and your family / Did / watch / TV last night?
____

3 you / Did / meet / your friends at the weekend?
____

4 you / help / Did / your parents this morning?
____

▸ Check

Erklärfilm

Das simple past: Fragen mit Fragewörtern

Auch Fragen mit Fragewörtern bildest du mit *did*. Das Fragewort steht immer am Satzanfang.

Fragewort	did	Person	Verb im Infinitiv		
Where	*did*	*Lily*	*take*	*the photo?*	*(Wo hat Lily das Foto gemacht?)*
When	*did*	*she*	*take*	*the photo?*	*(Wann hat sie das Foto gemacht?)*

► SB p. 47, p. 175

4 Isla's holiday

Write the right question words in Livia's questions. Tip: Read Isla's answers first.
Schreibe die richtigen Fragewörter in Livias Fragen. Tipp: Lies zuerst Islas Antworten.

who? – wer?
what? – was?
when? – wann?
where? – wo?
why? – warum?
how? – wie?

how • what • when • ~~where~~ • who

Livia (1) Where ____________ did you go on holiday?
Isla We went to Lake Garda in Italy.
Livia Nice! (2) ____________ did you get there?
Isla We went there by train.
Livia (3) ____________ did you go with?
Isla I went with my dad, my sister and my cousin.
Livia (4) ____________ did you do there?
Isla We did lots of things! We rode our bikes, we went swimming – and we ate pizzas!
Livia That sounds amazing. (5) ____________ did you get home?
Isla We got home in the last week of the holidays.

5 Where did you meet your friends?

Write questions with the words in the right order.
Schreibe Fragen mit den Wörtern in der richtigen Reihenfolge.

1 meet / your friends? / did / Where / you ____________
2 phone / Sunita / did / last night? / Who ____________
3 did / What / have / in his lunch box? / he ____________
4 Emma / write / Why / did / a poem? ____________
5 finish / your homework? / did / you / When ____________

► Check

Nebensätze mit Konjunktionen

Konjunktionen verwendest du, um Sätze miteinander zu verknüpfen. Die Wortstellung im Hauptsatz und im Nebensatz nach der Konjunktion ist immer gleich: subject – verb – object.

subject	verb	object	Konjunktion	subject	verb	object
I	*have*	*a snack*	*when*	*I*	*'m*	*hungry.*
They	*got*	*the bus*	*because*	*they*	*didn't want*	*to walk.*

► SB p. 68, p. 176

6 Milo missed the bus

Read the conversation. Circle the right words. *Lies die Unterhaltung. Kreise die richtigen Wörter ein.*

because – weil
when – als

Farah Hi, Milo! What's up?

Milo I'm very unhappy because / when I missed the bus.

Farah Oh, no. What happened?

Milo I left home a bit late because / when I couldn't find my sport bag. Because / When I got to High Street, I heard the bus and I started to run really fast. But because / when I arrived at the bus stop, the bus driver drove away because / when she didn't see me!

7 Because I can't

Complete the sentences. *Vervollständige die Sätze.*

1 We can't go to the cinema because *we don't have any money* .
don't have / we / any money

2 I can't talk for long because ______________________ .
I / have / lots of homework

3 Dinner will be ready when ______________________ .
you / home / get

4 I watched films in English when ______________________ .
wanted to become / better in English / I

5 I downloaded his new album because ______________________ .
in the car / want to play / I / it

► Check

8 Revision Quiz

a) **Complete the questions with the words from the box.**
Vervollständige die Fragen mit den Wörtern aus dem Kasten.

did (2x) • when • write

1 Where did ______ the 2024 Olympic Games take place?

2 Which famous book did Lewis Caroll ______?

3 ______ did Germany last win the FIFA World Cup?

4 Which well-known song ______ DJ Robin & Schürze make in 2022?

b) **Can you answer the questions? You can check your answers online.**
Kannst du die Fragen beantworten? Du kannst deine Lösungen im Internet überprüfen.

1 ______

2 ______

3 ______

4 ______

9 Revision Find the mistakes

There's one mistake in each sentence. Write the correct sentence.
In jedem Satz gibt es einen Fehler. Schreibe den korrekten Satz.

Achte auf das *simple past* und die Konjunktionen in diesen Sätzen.

1 Where you went on holiday?
Where did you go on holiday?

2 I walked to school this morning when it was a nice day.
______

3 You started school late yesterday?
______

4 What you did buy at the shops?
______

5 Did you see the cat because you got home last night?
______

► Check

Unit 3
Activities and games

Erklär-film

Das Futur mit going to

Mit *going to* sagst du, dass du etwas in der Zukunft plantst (*after school, tomorrow, next week*).
I'm going to bedeutetet „Ich werde" oder „Ich habe vor".

I'm going to go to a holiday camp this summer. (Ich werde diesen Sommer in ein Ferienlager fahren.)
My parents aren't going to buy a new car this year. (Meine Eltern haben nicht vor, dieses Jahr ein neues Auto zu kaufen.)
Is Holly going to visit her grandma tomorrow? (Wird Holly morgen ihre Großmutter besuchen?)

► SB p. 73, pp. 176–177

1 Alma's blog

a) **Read Alma's blog.** *Lies Almas Blog.*

www.almasblog.example.com

We're going to have an activity week at our school next week. There are going to be 30 activities and we can choose two. I love sport, so I'm going to choose football. Karate sounds good too, but I'm not going to do two sports activities. I'd like to try something creative, so I'm going to try a screen printing workshop. My friends aren't going to do the same as me. Anita is going to do chess club and photography. Felix is going to study local history and photography. Activity week is going to be fun!

screen printing

b) **Read Alma's blog again. Are the sentences true (T) or false (F).**
Lies Alma's Blog noch einmal. Sind die Sätze richtig oder falsch?

1 Activity week is going to be next week. ☐
2 Alma is going to choose two sports activities. ☐
3 Alma and Anita are going to do the same activities. ☐
4 Anita and Felix are going to do photography. ☐
5 Alma is going to enjoy activity week. ☐

► Check

2 Interview questions

Read the interview questions and write Alma's answers from the box.
Lies die Interviewfragen und schreibe Almas Antworten aus dem Kasten.

Footie Fans. • In the park. • Because I love football! • Our PE teacher. • Next week. • It isn't going to cost anything.

1 *Which activity are you going to choose?* ______________________

2 *Who is going to plan the activity?* ______________________

3 *Where are you going to do the activity?* ______________________

4 *When is it going to start?* ______________________

5 *How much is it going to cost?* ______________________

6 *Why are you going to enjoy it?* ______________________

3 The friends' activity week plans

a) **Can you remember the four friends' plans? Circle the right answer.**
Kannst du dich an die Pläne der vier Freunde erinnern? Kreise die richtige Antwort ein.

1 Is Zane going to learn about photography? – Yes, he is. / No, he isn't.

2 Are Lily and Sunita going to do sports activities? – Yes, they are. / No, they aren't.

3 Is Noah going to study 'History in Brighton'? – Yes, he is. / No, he isn't.

4 Is Zane going to choose 'Tea party and show'? – Yes, he is. / No, he isn't.

5 Are Lily and Noah going to do creative activities? – Yes, they are. / No, they aren't.

b) **Look at page 73 in your Student's book to check your answers.**
Schau dir Seite 73 in deinem Schulbuch an und überprüfe deine Antworten.

▸ Check

Erklärfilm

Die Steigerung von Adjektiven: Komparativ

Mit den Steigerungsformen der Adjektive kannst du Dinge oder Personen miteinander vergleichen.

A Bei einsilbigen Adjektiven und zweisilbigen Adjektiven, die auf *-y* enden, hängst du *-er* an. Beachte die Schreibweise:

old	*older (than)*	*My mum is older than my dad.*
easy	*easier (than)*	*I think English is easier than French.*
big	*bigger (than)*	*Emre's dog is bigger than Nila's dog.*

B Hat das Adjektiv drei oder mehr Silben oder zwei Silben und endet nicht auf *-y*, steigerst du es mit more.

famous	*more famous (than)*	*Spiderman is more famous than Captain Planet.*
expensive	*more expensive (than)*	*A car is more expensive than a bike.*
interesting	*more interesting (than)*	*This book is more interesting than the others.*

▸ SB p. 77, p. 178

4 Superhero quiz

a) **Read the sentences and find out the superheroes' names. Write them under the pictures.**
Lies die Sätze und finde die Namen der Superhelden heraus. Schreibe sie unter die Bilder.

1 Lady Fight ____ 2 ____ 3 ____ 4 ____ 5 ____ 6 ____

1 Doctor Heart's cape is shorter than all the other capes.
2 Coolboy's hair is darker than Lady Fight's hair.
3 Captain Right is smaller than all the others.
4 Megastorm's hair is lighter than Captain Right's hair.
5 Mr Strong's mask is bigger than Captain Right and Megastorm's masks.

b) **Look at the adjectives in c). Highlight all adjectives with three and more syllables.**
Sieh dir die Adjective in c) an. Markiere alle Adjektive, die drei und mehr Silben haben.

c) **What do you think? Complete the sentences.**
Was meinst du? Vervollständige die Sätze.

1 Lady Fight is more energetic than Captain Right. (energetic)
2 Megastorm is ____ than ____. (dangerous)
3 Coolboy is ____ than ____. (cool)
4 Mr Strong is ____ than ____. (strong)
5 Doctor Heart is ____ than ____. (interesting)

▸ Check

5 Three superheroes' cars

Compare the superheroes' cars. Complete the sentences.
Vergleiche die Autos der Superhelden. Vervollständige die Sätze.

A

B

C

1 Car B is *newer than* ______ car A.
2 Car A is *more beautiful than* ______ car B.
3 Car C is ______ car A.
4 Car A is ______ car C.
5 Car B is ______ car C.
6 Car C is ______ car B.
7 Car C is ______ car A.

new
beautiful
fast
old
small
expensive
exciting

6 The same?

Some things are the same, some aren't. Write sentences with the adjectives from the box.
Einige Dinge sind gleich, einige sind es nicht. Schreibe Sätze mit den Adjektiven aus dem Kasten.

famous • relaxing • slow • ~~warm~~

Möchtest du sagen, dass etwas (nicht) genau gleich ist, verwendest du:

(not) as … as
as cool as (so cool wie)
not as expensive as (nicht so teuer wie)

1 Brighton is *as warm as* ______ London in summer.
2 Cars aren't ______ bikes.
3 Harry Styles is ______ the Beatles.
4 Rock music isn't ______ classical music.

► Check

Die Steigerung von Adjektiven: Superlativ

Erklär-film

Möchtest du sagen, dass etwas am besten, größten, teuersten usw. ist, verwendest du den Superlativ.

A Bei einsilbigen Adjektiven und zweisilbigen Adjektiven, die auf *-y* enden, hängst du *-est* an.
Beachte wieder die Schreibweise:

old	*the oldest*	*Dima is the oldest boy in class.*
funny	*the funniest*	*Megastorm is the funniest superhero.*
big	*the biggest*	*We live in the biggest house in the road.*

B Hat das Adjektiv drei oder mehr Silben oder zwei Silben und endet nicht auf *-y*,
bildest du den Superlativ mit *most*.

beautiful	*the most beautiful*	*Roses are the most beautiful flowers.*
important	*the most important*	*This is the most important competition of the year.*

► SB p. 78, p. 178

7 Holiday places

a) **Write the superlative.** *Schreibe den Superlativ.*

	comparative	superlative
1 expensive	more expensive	the most expensive
2 rainy	rainier	the
3 warm	warmer	
4 cold	colder	
5 popular	more popular	

b) **Look at the information and complete the sentences with the correct superlative from a).**
Schau dir die Informationen an und vervollständige dann die Sätze mit den Superlativen aus a).

1 Cork and Inverness are popular holiday places, but Brighton is the most popular ______ town.

2 Inverness isn't an expensive town. Brighton is more expensive and Cork is ______________

______________ town.

3 Inverness and Cork are warm in summer, but Brighton is ______________ town.

4 Cork isn't very cold in winter. Brighton is colder and Inverness is ______________ town.

5 Inverness isn't very rainy. Brighton is rainier and Cork is ______________ town.

► Check

8 This is the best!

Complete the sentences with the superlatives of the adjectives in brackets. *Vervollständige die Sätze mit den Superlativen der Adjektive in Klammern.*

Diese unregelmäßigen Steigerungsformen musst du lernen:
good – better – the best
bad – worse – the worst

1 Tom is the happiest __________ person in our family. (happy)

2 This is __________ day of my life! (bad)

3 Scout is __________ seagull on the beach! (noisy)

4 Dungeons & Dragons is __________ role-playing game. (exciting)

5 Is this __________ activity this week? (good)

6 I think knitting is __________ course in activity week. (creative)

9 Zane and his family

Complete Zane's text with the adjectives from the box in the superlative form. *Vervollständige Zanes Text mit dem Superlativ der Adjektive aus dem Kasten.*

active • long • old • tall • wonderful • young

I'm 12, but I'm not (1) __________ person in my family: my sister Holly is younger. She's seven.

Dad is 43. He's a bit older than Mum. He's (2) __________ person in the Adebayo family. Mum is 41.

I'm tall, but I'm not (3) __________ person in my family – yet! At the moment Dad is 3 cm taller than me.

Dad doesn't have hair and my hair is short, but Holly and Mum have long hair. Mum has (4) __________ hair in the family.

I love swimming. I'm always active – I'm (5) __________ person in the family.

My family is wonderful! I think we're (6) __________ family in the world!

► Check

BASIC

lighthouse 2

Grammarmaster

Lösungen

Cornelsen

Hello again! The last day of the holidays

1 REVISION A day on the beach

1 Sonya **is** playing volleyball. She **isn't** swimming.
2 Josh **isn't** standing on the beach. He**'s** surfing.
3 Ben and his dad **are** building a sandcastle. They **aren't** having a picnic.
4 Justine and her friend **are** taking a photo. They **aren't** sleeping.
5 Holly's dog **isn't** eating. It**'s** running for a ball.

Alle Lösungen aus diesem Heft findest du auch in deiner Cornelsen Lernen App.

Unit 1 Travel and holidays

1 How was your holiday?

Toby How was your holiday?
Lucy It **was** great, thanks. We **were** in Spain. Were you here in Brighton all the time?
Toby No, we **weren't**. We **were** in Wales for two weeks. It **was** cold and windy. Was the weather good in Spain?
Lucy It **was** sunny every day. The weather **was** perfect!

2 The first day back at school

1 Was Noah's shirt blue? - No, it **was** white.
2 Was Sunita's skirt black? - Yes, it **was**.
3 Were Noah and Zane's uniforms the same? - Yes, they **were**.

7 In the summer holidays

1 played • **2** travelled • **3** cycled • **4** enjoyed • **5** listened

4 Lisa's holiday

My parents were at work, so I **stayed** in Brighton in the holidays. I **visited** my grandma for some days. She's nice. She lives in Hove.
I often **cycled** to the beach. I **played** beach volleyball. Sometimes I **watched** a film at the cinema.
One night I was at Ravi's birthday party. We **talked**, **listened** to music and **danced**.
I **liked** the Pride Parade too. There were 300,000 people in Brighton that day.

5 Irregular verbs

a)
1 was/were • **2** bought • **3** ate • **4** heard • **5** made • **6** met • **7** sat • **8** took
b)
1 were • **2** heard • **3** did • **4** wrote • **5** bought • **6** ran • **7** sat • **8** met

6 Lily and Alice's holidays

Lily and her mum **flew** to Poland and **visited** Lily's aunt and uncle. They **did** lots of different things. One day they **took** her aunt and uncle's bikes and **went** around Krakow. They **had** lots of fun.
Alice **went** to Wales with her dad and her brother. It was a long journey – it **took** eight hours! They **were** on a campsite. It **was** a bit cold, but they **loved** it! In the evenings they **cooked** barbecues and they **sang** songs by the fire.

7 What about you?

((Lösungsbeispiel))

1 I talked to my grandma this morning.
2 I watched a film last weekend.
3 I played football yesterday.
4 I ate pizza last week.

8 Scout's summer (1)

a) b)

1 eat, didn't eat • **2** fly, didn't fly • **3** dance, didn't dance • **4** wear, didn't wear • **5** walk, didn't walk • **6** see, didn't see

9 Some mistakes

1 We **didn't** go to the football match last week. Was it good?
2 Your teacher didn't **give** you homework yesterday.
3 I didn't **know** about the party on Saturday night. Who was there?
4 It **didn't** rain last weekend.

10 Your last holidays

((Lösungsbeispiel))

On my last holiday my family and I flew to Spain. I bought a cool present for my friend Cem. I cooked a paella with my family. I didn't swim in a pool, but I swam in the sea.

11 REVISION Scout's summer (2)

Scout wasn't away in the holidays. She **was** in Brighton all summer. She **flew** around the city and she **enjoyed** the good weather. Scout **relaxed** on the beach and she **ate** a lot of food too. There **were** lots of tourists and some of them **gave** their fish and chips to Scout!

⊠ 12 REVISION Reasons why

1 We **didn't go** to the cinema last weekend because we **didn't have** time.
2 Ravi **didn't visit** us last weekend because he **didn't get** our invitation.
3 I **didn't finish** my pizza for lunch because I **wasn't** hungry.
4 The students **weren't** in class yesterday because it **wasn't** a school day.
5 I **didn't see** the Loch Ness Monster in Scotland because I **didn't go** to Loch Ness.

Unit 2 Friends and heroes

1 Yes, I did!

a) b)

1 **Did** she play football? – **Yes,** she **did.**
2 **Did** they walk to school? – **No,** they **didn't.**
3 **Did** he do the homework? – **Yes,** he **did.**
4 **Did** we go shopping? – **Yes,** we **did.**
5 **Did** you get the train? – **No,** I **didn't.**
6 **Did** she swim in the pool? – **No,** she **didn't.**

2 The friends' holidays

a)

1 **Did** Sunita's family **visit** Prague?
2 **Did** Sunita **stay** on a campsite?
3 **Did** Noah **go** on holiday to Wales?
4 **Did** Lily **travel** to Poland?
5 **Did** Zane's apartment **have** a pool?

b)

1 Yes, they did.	5 Yes, it did.	3 No, he didn't.	4 Yes, she did.	2 No, she didn't.

3 Did you ...?

1 Did you do sport last weekend? – Yes, I did.
2 Did you and your family watch TV last night? – Yes, we did. / No, we didn't.
3 Did you meet your friends at the weekend? – Yes, I did. / No, I didn't.
4 Did you help your parents this morning? – Yes, I did. / No, I didn't.

4 Isla's holiday

1 **Where** did you go on holiday?
2 **How** did you get there?
3 **Who** did you go with?
4 **What** did you do there?
5 **When** did you get home?

5 Where did you meet your friends?

1 Where did you meet your friends?
2 Who did Sunita phone last night?
3 What did he have in his lunch box?
4 Why did Emma write a poem?
5 When did you finish your homework?

6 Milo missed the bus

Farah Hi, Milo! What's up?
Milo I'm very unhappy **because** I missed the bus.
Farah Oh, no. What happened?
Milo I left home a bit late **because** I couldn't find my sport bag. **When** I got to High Street, I heard the bus and I started to run really fast. But **when** I arrived at the bus stop, the bus driver drove away **because** she didn't see me!

7 Because I can't

1 We can't go to the cinema because we don't have any money.
2 I can't talk for long because I have lots of homework.
3 Dinner will be ready when you get home.
4 I watched films in English when I wanted to become better in English.
5 I downloaded his new album because I want to play it in the car.

8 REVISION Quiz

a)

1 Where **did** the 2024 Olympic Games take place?
2 Which famous book did Lewis Caroll **write**?
3 **When** did Germany last win the FIFA World Cup?
4 **Which** well-known song **did** DJ Robin & Schürze make in 2022?

b)

1 In France. • **2** Alice in Wonderland. • **3** In 2014. • **4** Layla.

9 REVISION Find the mistakes

1 Where **did** you **go** on holiday?
2 I walked to school this morning **because** it was a nice day.
3 **Did you start** school late yesterday?
4 What **did you** buy at the shops?
5 Did you see the cat **when** you got home last night?

Unit 3 Activities and games

1 Alma's blog

b)

1 T • 2 F • 3 F • 4 T • 5 T

2 Interview questions

1 Footie Fans.
2 Our PE teacher.
3 In the park.
4 Next week.
5 It isn't going to cost anything.
6 Because I love football.

3 The friends' activity week plans

a)

1 No, he isn't.
2 No, they aren't.
3 No, he isn't.
4 Yes, he is.
5 Yes, they are.

4 Superhero quiz

a)

1 Lady Fight • **2** Megastorm • **3** Mr Strong • **4** Captain Right • **5** Dr Heart • **6** Coolboy

c)

((Lösungsbeispiel))

1 Lady Fight is **more energetic** than Captain Right.
2 Megastorm is **more dangerous** than Coolboy.
3 Coolboy is **cooler** than Dr Heart.
4 Mr Strong is **stronger** than Megastorm.
5 Doctor Heart is **more interesting** than Mr Strong.

5 Three superheroes' cars

1 newer than • **2** more beautiful than • **3** faster than • **4** older than • **5** smaller than • **6** more expensive than • **7** more exciting than

6 The same?

1 Brighton is **as warm as** London in summer.
2 Cars aren't **as slow as** bikes.
3 Harry Styles is **as famous as** the Beatles.
4 Rock music isn't **as relaxing as** classical music.

7 Holiday places

a)

1 the most expensive • **2** the rainiest • **3** the warmest • **4** the coldest • **5** the most popular

b)

1 Cork and Inverness are popular holiday places, but Brighton is **the most popular** town.
2 Inverness isn't an expensive town. Brighton is more expensive and Cork is **the most expensive** town.
3 Inverness and Cork are warm in summer, but Brighton is **the warmest** town.
4 Cork isn't very cold in winter. Brighton is colder and Inverness is **the coldest** town.
5 Inverness isn't very rainy. Brighton is rainier and Cork is **the rainiest** town.

8 This is the best!

1 the happiest • **2** the worst • **3** the noisiest • **4** the most exciting • **5** the best • **6** the most creative

9 Zane and his family

I'm 12, but I'm not **the youngest** person in my family: my sister Holly is younger. She's seven.
My Dad is 43. He's a bit older than Mum. He's **the oldest** person in the Adebayo family. Mum is 41.
I'm tall, but I'm not **the tallest** person in my family – yet! At the moment Dad is 3 cm taller than me.
Dad doesn't have hair and my hair is short, but Holly and Mum have long hair. Mum has **the longest** hair in the family.
I love swimming. I'm always active – I'm **the most active** person in the family.
My family is wonderful! I think we're **the most wonderful** family in the world!

10 Revision Weekend plans

1 good • **2** most • **3** the • **4** than • **5** as

11 REVISION True for you

((Lösungsbeispiel))
My phone is faster than my friend's phone.
My mum is older than my dad.
Weekends are more relaxing than school days.

Unit 4 Celebrate!

1 There are some peppers

1 some • **2** some • **3** any • **4** any • **5** some • **6** any

2 At the supermarket

1 some • **2** some • **3** any • **4** any • **5** some • **6** any

3 Breakfast at the restaurant

a)
1 some • **2** some • **3** some • **4** any • **5** some • **6** any • **7** some • **8** Some
b)
1 ✓ • 2 ✓ • 3 ✓ • 4 ✗ • 5 ✗ • 6 ✓

4 A little or a few?

a little	a few
a little money	*a few apples*
a little music	*a few books*
a little salad	*a few people*
a little sugar	*a few tickets*

5 Planning for a party

1 a little • **2** a few • **3** a little • **4** a few • **5** a few • **6** a few

6 At Emma's party

Lily Hi, Emma! Is there **anywhere** to put the snacks?
Emma Yes, just put them on the table over there. Would you like **something** to drink?
Lily Yes, please. Could I have some juice please?
Emma Sure. Would you like **something** to eat too?
Lily Hmm. I don't want **anything** sweet like cake. I think I'd like **something** with vegetables. Is there any salad?
Emma Sorry, there isn't **anything** with vegetables. But there is some fruit salad.
Lily Fruit salad, great!

7 Later on at Emma's party

1 something • **2** anything • **3** somewhere • **4** anywhere • **5** anybody • **6** somebody

8 The end of Ramadan

b)

1 Yes, he has.
2 Yes, they have.
3 No, she hasn't.
4 Yes, he has.
5 Yes, they have.

9 A few days before Meera and Ben's wedding

Meera and Ben have **planned** a big wedding near the beach. Ben has **made** a song for Meera. Meera has **invited** Zane and Noah. Sunita's grandparents have **flown** to the UK from India and her aunt and uncle from Birmingham have **arrived** in Brighton too. Sunita and Nish have **helped** their mum with the chores. Sunita has **played** games with her cousin.

10 Matching

1 Yes, I have.
2 No, it hasn't.
3 Yes, she has.
4 No, we haven't.
5 Yes, they have.
6 No, he hasn't.

11 REVISION Some, any, a little or a few?

1 a little • **2** a few • **3** any • **4** a little • **5** some • **6** any

12 REVISION Anything good?

1 **Some**one • **2** some**thing** • **3** some**where** • **4** **any**thing • **5** any**one** • **6** **some**thing

☒ 13 REVISION Crossword

								2	
		1	P	L	A	Y	E	D	
			L					E	
	3	M	A	D	E			C	
			N					O	
			N		4			R	
			E		G			A	
5	H	A	D		O			T	
				6	T	A	K	E	N
								D	

Unit 5 Getting ready for the future

1 Future jobs
1 'll work • **2** won't be • **3** 'll work • **4** 'll be • **5** won't become • **6** 'll work

2 Lily says
1 I **won't** play tennis this weekend. **I'll** play in the park.
2 Mum and I **will** go to Poland. We **won't** go on holiday to Germany.
3 Chloe's cat **will** sleep on the sofa. It **won't** sleep in Chloe's garden.
4 **I'll / will** draw some manga characters. I **won't** draw real people.
5 Chloe is 23 now. She**'ll / will** be 24 next year. She **won't** be 25.
6 My dad **won't** drive a bus tomorrow. He**'ll / will** drive a van.

3 I think it'll be ...
1 It won't rain tomorrow. I think it'll be sunny.
2 My sister won't / will not be at home later. I'm sure she'll / will go out with her friends.
3 I won't / will not babysit on Saturday. Maybe I'll /will go to the cinema with Samuel.
4 Mum's new job will be fun. I bet it won't / will not be boring!

4 Will you ...?
((Individuelle Lösungen))

5 Fifty years from now
1 E • **2** A • **3** B • **4** D • **5** C

6 Question words
1 Where • **2** What • **3** Who • **4** How

7 Tim's dream job
a)
1 **Will** you **work**
2 **Will** you **use**
3 **Will** you **need**
4 Where **will** your office **be**?
5 **Will** your job **be**
6 When **will** you **work**
b)
Tim will be a **musician**.

8 Parts of speech
1 a mechanic: Objekt • **2** went: Verb • **3** next week: Zeitangabe • **4** Mum: Subjekt •
5 at my house: Ortsangabe; at 8.30: Zeitangabe

9 Ordering
1 I wasn't at the supermarket.
2 I save my pocket money.
3 After dinner we helped Mum and Dad in the kitchen.
4 ... because I'll babysit my little cousin this weekend.
5 ... when she works for an animal charity.

10 My aunt's new cafe

1 My aunt wants to open a cafe at the beach next month.
2 So she has a lot of things to prepare at the cafe every day.
3 She works very hard in her cafe every day.
4 She comes home late every night.

11 Our jobs at home

1 She **always** empties the dishwasher.
2 I **often** vacuum the floor in my room.
3 We **sometimes** clean the garage with Dad.
4 It's **always** fun to look after our pets.
5 We **often** fold clean clothes.

12 REVISION Talking about jobs

Ms Bond This afternoon **we'll talk** about jobs you'd like to do one day. Liam, what will you do when you're older? Will you be a teacher like me?
Liam I love school, but I **won't work** in a school when I'm older. I think I'**ll get** a job as a nurse.
Ms Bond I'm sure you'**ll be** a brilliant nurse, Liam.
Liam Thank you.
Ms Bond Emma, what about you?
Emma I love art so I think I'**ll become** an artist. Will I have to go to university to be an artist?
Ms Bond No, some artists go to university and some don't. But don't worry, you **won't need** to think about university until you're much older.

13 REVISION What will you do?

((Lösungsbeispiel))
I think I'll live in a different country. Maybe I'll become a nurse. I'll have a big family. I'm sure I'll have a dog, but I won't have a fast car.

14 REVISION What's wrong?

1 ... because I was on a school trip.
2 My brother saved a lot of money ...
3 ... because she always likes to help people.
4 ... because I'll go to my friend's house after school.
5 Samir often babysits his cousin ...

☒ 15 REVISION Jumbled sentences

1 We won't / will not go to our guitar lesson tomorrow.
2 Will you be at the football match on Saturday?
3 Peter will meet his friends at the youth club this afternoon.
4 I'll / will become an architect one day.
5 What will you do next weekend?
6 Will Mum and Dad wait for us at school at 3 o'clock?

10 REVISION Weekend plans

Complete the conversation with the words from the box.
Vervollständige die Unterhaltung mit den Wörtern aus dem Kasten.

as • good • most • than • the

The Shard

Leon What are you going to do this weekend?

Carin I'm going to help my dad in the garden. It isn't going to be as (1) ____________________ as a day out with you guys, but it isn't going to be bad. What about you?

Leon My family and I are going to visit London.

Carin Are you going to visit famous places?

Leon Yes, I am. I'm going to go to the Shard. It's one of the (2) ____________________ popular tourist attractions in London. And it's one of (3) ____________________ tallest buildings in Western Europe.

Carin Is it taller (4) ____________________ the Eiffel Tower?

Leon No, it isn't (5) ____________________ tall as that.

11 REVISION True for you

Write three sentences about you.
Schreibe drei Sätze über dich.

<table>
<tr><td>I</td><td>'m</td><td rowspan="3">better
cooler
faster
nicer
older
slower
taller
worse
more boring
more exciting
more interesting
more relaxing</td><td rowspan="3">than</td><td rowspan="3">...</td></tr>
<tr><td>My sister / family / teacher / dog ...
My phone / hair / school / ...</td><td>is</td></tr>
<tr><td>My friends / grandparents / ...
Weekends / Holidays / Books / Films / ...</td><td>are</td></tr>
</table>

____

____

____

▶ Check

Unit 4
Celebrate!

Some / any

Erklär-film

Wenn du über eine Menge oder Anzahl sprechen möchtest, du diese Menge oder Anzahl aber nicht genau kennst, verwendest du im Englischen *some* und *any*.

some
- bedeutet „einige", „etwas"
- in bejahten Sätzen
- wenn du um etwas bittest
- wenn du etwas anbietest

Zane invited some friends. (einige Freunde)
Can I have some biscuits, please? (einige Kekse)
Would you like some water? (etwas Wasser)

any
- bedeutet „kein", „keine", „keinen"
- in verneinten Sätzen
- in Fragen

My parents and I don't eat any meat. (kein Fleisch)
Are there any chairs in the classroom? (keine Stühle)

► SB p. 101, p. 179

1 There are some peppers

Look at the pictures and circle the correct words. *Sieh dir die Bilder an und kreise die richtigen Wörter ein.*

1

There's some / any cake.

2

There are some / any fireworks.

3

There aren't some / any tomatoes.

4

There isn't some / any water.

5

There's some / any milk.

6

There aren't some / any lemons.

► Check

2 At the supermarket

Emma is at the supermarket. Look at her shopping list and complete her sentences with *some* or *any*.
Emma ist im Supermarkt. Schau dir ihre Einkaufsliste an und vervollständige ihre Sätze mit some *oder* any.

Right. I have (1) some *flour and I have (2)________ sugar. I don't have (3)________ bananas and I don't have (4)________ chocolate. I have (5)________ yoghourt, but there aren't (6)________ eggs.*

Shopping List

- [x] ~~flour~~
- [x] ~~yoghurt~~
- [ ] eggs
- [ ] chocolate
- [x] ~~sugar~~
- [ ] bananas

3 Breakfast at the restaurant

Angebot: *Would you like some bread?*
Bitte: *Can I have some toast, please?*

a) **Read the conversation and complete it with *some* or *any*.**
Lies die Unterhaltung und vervollständige sie mit some *oder* any.

Waiter[1] Good morning. Would you like (1)________ juice?

Elias Yes, please. And can my sister have (2)________ water, please?

Waiter Of course. Would you like (3)________ toast?

Elias Yes, please, but we don't need (4)________ butter. We'd just like (5)________ cheese, please.

Waiter I'm sorry, there isn't (6)________ cheese. But we have (7)________ ham.

Elias (8)________ ham would be perfect, thank you!

b) **Read the conversation in a) again. What do Elias and his sister have for breakfast? Put a tick (✓) or a cross (✗).** *Lies die Unterhaltung in a) noch einmal. Was essen und trinken Elias und seine Schwester zum Frühstück? Mache ein Häkchen oder ein Kreuz.*

1

2

3

4

5

6

► Check

[1] **waiter** *der Kellner*

Erklärfilm

A little / a few

Du weißt schon, wie du über große Mengen sprechen kannst. Du verwendest dafür *much* für nicht zählbare Dinge und *many* für zählbare Dinge. Möchtest du aber über kleine Mengen sprechen, verwendest du a little und a few.

a little
- bedeutet „ein wenig", „etwas"
- bei nicht zählbaren Nomen, das heißt, du kannst von diesen Nomen keinen Plural bilden *(water, juice, music, love, money)*

I need a little fruit for my cake. (ein wenig Obst)
Can I have a little sugar for my tea, please? (etwas Zucker)

a few
- bedeutet „einige", „ein paar"
- bei zählbaren Nomen, das heißt, du kannst einen Plural bilden *(one apple, two apples)*

There were a few mistakes in your test. (einige Fehler)
There are only a few strawberries left. (ein paar Erdbeeren)

▶ SB p. 102, p. 179

4 A little or a few?

Write the words from the box into the right list. Write them with *a little* and *a few*. *Schreibe die Wörter aus dem Kasten in die richtige Liste. Schreibe sie mit* a little *und* a few.

Are the words in the box singular or plural?

apples • books • ~~money~~ • music • people • salad • sugar • tickets

a little	a few
a little money	

5 Planning for a party

Read the conversation and complete it with *a little* and *a few*.
Lies die Unterhaltung und vervollständige sie mit a little *und* a few.

Lily What can we take to Emma's party?

Finn We could take (1)_____________ food.

Lily Good idea. I can take (2)_____________ snacks.

Sunita And I can make (3)_____________ lemonade!

Noah My mum is going to make (4)_____________ pizzas.

Lily That sounds great. What about music?

Zane I can play (5)_____________ songs on my guitar if you like?
And I can bring (6)_____________ games too.

▶ Check

Zusammensetzungen mit *some* und *any*

- In bejahten Aussagesätzen verwendest du: *somebody/someone, something, somewhere*
  There's somebody in the house. (Da ist jemand im Haus.)
  I can do something nice for my mum. (Ich kann etwas Schönes für meine Mutter machen.)
  My friend is somewhere in the classroom. (Mein Freund ist irgendwo im Klassenraum.)
- In verneinten Aussagesätzen und Fragen verwendest du: *anybody/anyone, anything, anywhere*
  Is there anybody at school today? (Ist heute jemand in der Schule?)
  There isn't anything to eat! (Es gibt nichts zu essen.)
  Can you see my phone anywhere? (Kannst du irgendwo mein Telefon sehen?)

▶ SB p. 109, p. 181

6 At Emma's party

Read the conversation and circle the correct words.
Lies die Unterhaltung und kreise die richtigen Wörter ein.

Bei Angeboten und Bitten verwendest du *some, somebody/someone, something, somewhere*:
Would you like something to drink? (Möchtest du etwas zu trinken?)

Lily Hi, Emma! Is there anywhere / anything to put the snacks?

Emma Yes, just put them on the table over there. Would you like something / somebody to drink?

Lily Yes, please. Could I have some juice please?

Emma Sure. Would you like somewhere / something to eat too?

Lily Hmm. I don't want anything / anybody sweet like cake.
I think I'd like somebody / something with vegetables. Is there any salad?

Emma Sorry, there isn't anything / anywhere with vegetables. But there's some fruit salad.

Lily Fruit salad, great!

7 Later on at Emma's party

Complete the sentences with the words on the right. *Vervollständige die Sätze mit den Wörtern rechts.*

Finn Is there (1)__________________ I can help you with, Emma?
Emma No, thanks. There isn't (2)__________________ to do.

anything / something

Noah Let's go (3)__________________ quiet. It's noisy here.
Emma Sorry, there isn't (4)__________________ quiet.

anywhere / somewhere

Zane Did (5)__________________ see my guitar? I need
(6)__________________ to tell me where I can find it.

anybody / somebody

▶ Check

Erklär-film

Das present perfect

Mit dem *present perfect* sagst du, dass jemand irgendwann etwas getan hat oder dass irgendwann etwas geschehen ist. Der genaue Zeitpunkt des Geschehens ist unwichtig oder unbekannt.

We've played basketball a lot of times. (Wir haben oft Basketball gespielt.)
Mara hasn't visited Brighton. (Mara ist nicht in Brighton gewesen.)
Have you finished your homework? – Yes, I have. (Hast du deine Hausaufgaben gemacht? – Ja, habe ich.)

! Manche Verben haben eine besondere Form.

Ahmet has been to Scotland very often. (Ahmet ist oft in Schottland gewesen.)
My parents haven't had a car yet. (Meine Eltern haben noch kein Auto gehabt.)
Has Louisa met Paolo? – Yes, she has. (Hat Louisa Paolo getroffen? – Ja, hat sie.) ▸ SB p. 105, pp. 180–181, p. 271

8 The end of Ramadan

a) **Read the text about Zane's dad.**
Lies den Text über Zanes Vater.

Eno Adebayo has fasted for the month of Ramadan. During the day, Eno hasn't had a drink and he hasn't eaten anything. Zane, Holly and their mum Louise haven't fasted, but they have helped Eno. Soon they are going to celebrate Eid al-Fitr, the end of Ramadan. Zane has given invitations to the Eid celebration to his friends. The Adebayos have celebrated Eid every year – and Zane and Holly have got lots of presents!

b) **Read the questions and circle the correct answer.**
Lies die Fragen und kreise die richtige Antwort ein.

1 Has Eno Adebayo fasted for Ramadan? – Yes, he has. / No, he hasn't.
2 Have Zane and Holly eaten during the day? – Yes, they have. / No, they haven't.
3 Has Louise Adebayo fasted? – Yes, she has. / No, she hasn't.
4 Has Zane invited his friends to Eid al-Fitr? – Yes, he has. / No, he hasn't.
5 Have Zane and Holly got presents? – Yes, they have. / No, they haven't.

▸ Check

9 A few days before Meera and Ben's wedding

Meera and Ben want to get married. Complete the sentences with the words from the box.
Meera und Ben wollen heiraten. Vervollständige die Sätze mit den Wörtern aus dem Kasten.

arrived • flown • helped • invited • made • ~~planned~~ • played

Meera and Ben have (1) planned __________ a big wedding near the beach. Ben has (2) __________ a song for Meera. Meera has (3) __________ Zane and Noah. Sunita's grandparents have (4) __________ to the UK from India and her aunt and uncle from Birmingham have (5) __________ in Brighton too. Sunita and Nish have (6) __________ their mum with the chores. Sunita has (7) __________ games with her cousin.

10 Matching

Read the questions and write the right answers from the box.
Lies die Fragen und schreibe die richtigen Antworten aus dem Kasten.

~~Yes, I have.~~ • Yes, she has. • Yes, they have. • No, it hasn't. • No, he hasn't. • No, we haven't.

1 *Have you found your classroom?*	Yes, I have.
2 *Has the rain stopped?*	__________
3 *Has your sister taken her judo test?*	__________
4 *Have you or Mum seen my pen anywhere?*	__________
5 *Have they left the cinema?*	__________
6 *Has Leon played the guitar?*	__________

▸ Check

11 REVISION Some, any, a little or a few?

Read the family's sentences. Circle the right words.
Lies die Sätze der Familienmitglieder. Kreise die richtigen Wörter ein.

1 I've just eaten a little / a few chocolate.
2 Can I eat a little / a few of your sausages?
3 There aren't any / some apples on the table.
4 Could I have a little / a few more juice, please?
5 There's any / some bread.
6 Dad doesn't like any / some bananas.

12 REVISION Anything good?

Complete the words. *Vervollständige die Wörter.*

any • one • some (2x) • thing • where

1 ____________ one has taken my money!
2 I'm going to tell you some ____________, but it's a secret.
3 Can you think of some ____________ fun to go to this weekend?
4 I don't want to do ____________ thing this evening.
5 Has any ____________ seen my phone?
6 Would you like to do ____________ thing special this weekend?

☒ 13 REVISION Crossword

Fill the crossword with the past participles of the verbs.
Vervollständige das Kreuzworträtsel mit der 3. Form der Verben.

Across →
1 I haven't (play) this song.
3 Have you (make) the cake?
5 Lily has (have) lunch.
6 Someone has (take) my bag!

Down ↓
1 The class has (plan) their next trip.
2 Has Marc (decorate) the room?
4 Peter has (get) a new phone.

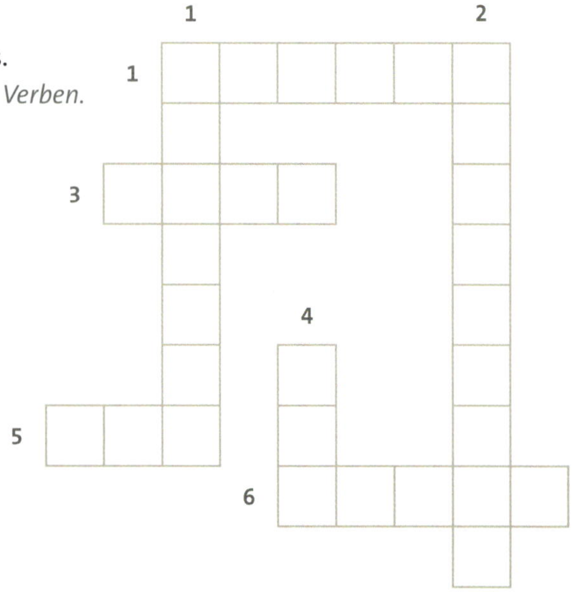

► Check

Unit 5
Getting ready for the future

Erklär-
film

Das will-future: Bejahte und verneinte Aussagesätze

Du verwendest das *will-future*, wenn du sagen willst, was in der Zukunft wahrscheinlich geschehen wird.
Oft verwendest du es mit *I think, maybe, I'm sure*.

A **Bejahte Aussagesätze**

I / you / he / she / it / we / you / they	will / 'll	+ Grundform des Verbs	*I think we'll stay at home tomorrow. It'll be rainy. (Ich denke, wir werden morgen zu Hause bleiben. Es wird regnerisch.)*

B **Verneinte Aussagesätze**

I / you / he / she / it / we / you / they	will not / won't	+ Grundform des Verbs	*I'm sure I won't become a programmer. (Ich bin sicher, dass ich kein Programmierer werde.)*

► SB p. 132, p. 182

1 Future jobs

Look at the pictures. What are the Varndean students' future job plans? Circle the right words.
Schau dir die Bilder an. Welche Berufspläne haben die Kinder von Varndean? Kreise die richtigen Wörter ein.

1

Ava: animal charity

In the future, I 'll work / won't work for an animal charity.

2

Lily: firefighter

I 'll be / won't be a police officer.

3

Noah: vet

I think I 'll work / won't work as a vet.

4

Sunita: gamer

I hope I 'll be / won't be a professional gamer.

5

Zane: cook

Maybe I 'll become / won't become a professional footballer.

6

Finn: programmer

I'm sure I 'll work / won't work as a programmer.

► Check

2 Lily says

Look at the pictures and complete Lily's sentences with *will/'ll or won't*.
Sieh dir die Bilder an und vervollständige Lilys Sätze mit will/'ll *oder* won't.

1

I *won't* play tennis this weekend. I *'ll* play in the park.

2

Mum and I ________ go to Poland. We ________ go on holiday to Germany.

3
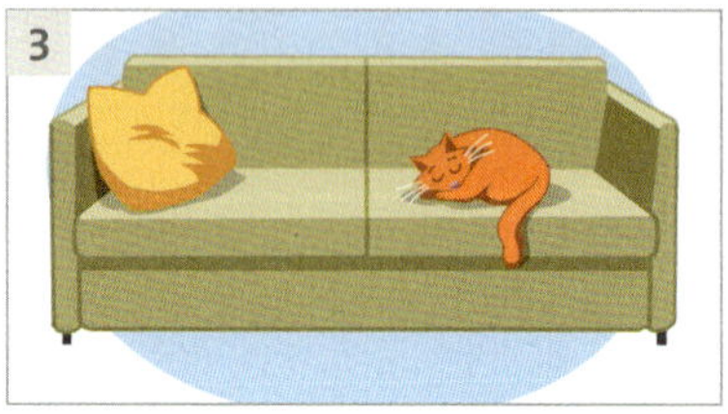

Chloe's cat ________ sleep on the sofa. It ________ sleep in Chloe's garden.

4

I ________ draw some manga characters. I ________ draw real people.

5

Chloe is 23 now.
She ________ be 24 next year.
She ________ be 25.

6

My dad ________ drive a bus tomorrow.
He ________ drive a van.

3 I think it'll be ...

Write sentences. *Schreibe Sätze.*

1 It / not rain / tomorrow. / I think it / be / sunny.
It won't rain tomorrow. I think it'll be sunny.

2 My sister / not be / at home later. / I'm sure she / go / out with her friends.
____

3 I / not babysit / on Saturday. / Maybe I / go / to the cinema with Samuel.
____

4 Mum's new job / be / fun. / I bet it / not be / boring!
____

► Check

Erklär-
film

Das will-future: Fragen und Kurzantworten

Bei Fragen im *will-future* steht *will* am Satzanfang. Hat die Frage ein Fragewort, steht das noch davor.

Will your sister be at the party? – Yes, she will. (Wird deine Schwester auf der Party sein? – Ja, wird sie.)
Will you meet Oscar tomorrow? – No, I won't. (Wirst du Oscar morgen treffen? – Nein, werde ich nicht.)
When will she arrive? – At 8 o'clock. (Wann wird sie ankommen? – Um 8 Uhr.)
Where will we meet? – In front of the cinema. (Wo werden wir uns treffen? – Vor dem Kino.)

► SB p. 132, p. 182

4 Will you …?

Read the questions and tick (✓) the answers that are true for you.
Lies die Fragen und mache ein Häkchen (✓) bei der Antwort, die auf dich zutrifft.

1 Will you go to the park this weekend? ☐ Yes, I will. ☐ No, I won't.
2 Will you get a job next summer? ☐ Yes, I will. ☐ No, I won't.
3 Will you watch TV in the evening? ☐ Yes, I will. ☐ No, I won't.
4 Will you see your grandparents this week? ☐ Yes, I will. ☐ No, I won't.
5 Will you ride your bike to school tomorrow? ☐ Yes, I will. ☐ No, I won't.

5 Fifty years from now

Match the questions and answers and write the right letters A–E in the boxes.
Ordne die Fragen und Antworten zu und schreibe die richtigen Buchstaben A–E in die Kästchen.

1 What will jobs be like?	*A I think people will have flying cars.*
2 How will people travel around?	*B Maybe it'll be hotter.*
3 What will the weather be like?	*C We'll do some, but robots will cook and make beds.*
4 Will robots teach in schools?	*D No, they won't. Schools will have real teachers!*
5 Will we do the chores at home?	*E I'm sure everyone will use computers in their jobs.*

1 ☐ 2 ☐ 3 ☐ 4 ☐ 5 ☐

► Check

6 Question words

Complete the questions with *How, What, Where* or *Who*.
Vervollständige die Fragen mit How, What, Where *oder* Who.

1 ____________ will you go on holiday this summer?
– I don't know. Maybe to Turkey or to Spain.

2 ____________ will you read next?
– I'm not sure. Do you know a good book?

3 ____________ will come to your party?
– I haven't invited anyone yet. Would you like to come?

4 ____________ will you get to the park?
– I think I'll ride my bike.

Remember:
how? – wie?
what? – was?
where? – wo?
who? – wer?

7 Tim's dream job

a) **Write interview questions with the verbs in brackets.**
Schreibe Interviewfragen mit den Verben in Klammern.

Alisha (1) Will ____________ you work ____________ (work) with people?
Tim Yes, I will. I'll work with people and for people.
Alisha (2) ____________ you ____________ (use) a computer?
Tim Yes, I think I'll need one sometimes.
Alisha (3) ____________ you ____________ (need) a car?
Tim Yes, I'll need a car to travel with all my instruments.
Alisha (4) Where ____________ your office ____________ (be)?
Tim I won't have an office. I'll work in clubs, concert halls, maybe in stadiums too.
Alisha (5) ____________ your job ____________ (be) fun?
Tim Oh, yes! I hope it will be lots of fun.
Alisha (6) When ____________ you ____________ (work), at day or at night?
Tim At day and at night. I'll practise during the day and I'll work in the evenings.

b) **What's Tim's dream job?** *Was ist Tims Traumberuf?*

Tim will be a ______________________________.

s i m u c a i n

► Check

Die Wortstellung

Im englischen Aussagesatz ist die Wortstellung immer subject – verb – object:

I meet my friends when we play football together.

Eine Ortsangabe steht meist nach Verb und Objekt.

Subjekt	Verb	Objekt	Ort
I	*meet*	*my friends*	*at school.*

Zeitangaben stehen am Anfang oder am Ende des Satzes.

Zeit	Subjekt	Verb	Objekt	Zeit
Every day	*I*	*meet*	*my friends.*	
	I	*meet*	*my friends*	*every day.*

► SB p. 137, p. 182

8 Parts of speech

Read the sentences. What are the phrases in blue? *Lies die Sätze. Was sind die Satzglieder in Blau?*

1 I won't be a mechanic. — a mechanic: (Objekt) / Subjekt
2 They went for a bike ride yesterday. — went: Verb / Zeitangabe
3 It's my birthday next week. — next week: Ortsangabe / Zeitangabe
4 Mum is going to help us tomorrow. — Mum: Objekt / Subjekt
5 I'll meet you at my house at 8.30. — at my house: Objekt / Ortsangabe; at 8.30: Ortsangabe / Zeitangabe

9 Ordering

Write sentences. Put the words in the right order.
Schreibe Sätze. Bringe die Wörter in die richtige Reihenfolge.

1 at the supermarket. / I / wasn't
I wasn't at the supermarket.

2 save / I / my pocket money.
____

3 After dinner / we / Mum and Dad / in the kitchen. / helped
____

4 my little cousin / I / 'll babysit / this weekend.
I can't come to your party because ______________________________

5 she / for an animal charity. / works
She's always very happy when ______________________________

► Check

10 My aunt's new cafe

Write the sentence parts in the right place.
Schreibe die Satzteile an die richtige Stelle im Satz.

Stehen in einem Satz eine Orts- und eine Zeitangabe, kommt Ort vor Zeit.
Das ist wie im Alphabet: O kommt vor Z.
I meet my friends at school every day.

1 My aunt wants to open a cafe ______________________ at the beach / next month

2 So she has a lot of things to prepare ______________________ every day / at the cafe

3 She works very hard ______________________ in her cafe / every day

4 She comes ______________________ late every night / home

11 Our jobs at home

Write the sentences with the adverbs of frequency in the correct place.
Schreibe die Sätze mit den Häufigkeitsadverbien an der richtigen Stelle.

Häufigkeitsadverbien (*always, often, never, ...*) stehen immer vor dem Verb.
Marcus often plays the guitar.
I never eat meat.

! Ausnahme ist das Verb *be*. Hier steht das Häufigkeitsadverb dahinter.
I'm never late for school.

1 She empties the dishwasher. (always)
She always empties the dishwasher.

2 I vacuum the floor in my room. (often)
____

3 We clean the garage with Dad. (sometimes)
____

4 It's fun to look after our pets. (always)
____

5 We fold clean clothes. (often)
____

▸ Check

12 REVISION Talking about jobs

Complete the conversation with *'ll* or *won't* and the verbs in brackets.
Vervollständige die Unterhaltung mit 'll *oder* won't *und den Verben in Klammern.*

Ms Bond This afternoon we (1)____________________ (talk) about jobs you'd like to do one day. Liam, what will you do when you're older? Will you be a teacher like me?

Liam I love school, but I (2)____________________ (work) in a school when I'm older. I think I (3)____________________ (get) a job as a nurse.

Ms Bond I'm sure you (4)____________________ (be) a brilliant nurse, Liam.

Liam Thank you.

Ms Bond Emma, what about you?

Emma I love art so I think I (5)____________________ (become) an artist. Will I have to go to university to be an artist?

Ms Bond No, some artists go to university and some don't. But don't worry, you (6)____________________ (need) to think about university until you're much older.

13 REVISION What will you do?

Write four sentences about your future. What will or what won't you do when you have grown up? You can use the ideas in the box or your own ideas. *Schreibe vier Sätze über deine Zukunft. Was wirst du tun oder nicht tun, wenn du erwachsen bist? Du kannst die Ideen aus dem Kasten verwenden oder deine eigenen Ideen.*

I think I'm sure Maybe	I'll I won't	live	in a big city / in a small village / in a different country / in New York / ...
		become	a nurse / a police officer / a famous musician / a firefighter / a mechanic / a gamer / ...
		have	a big family / a cool house / a dog / a fast car / ...

____

____

____

____

► Check

☒ 14 REVISION What's wrong?

There's a mistake in each sentence. Find and correct it.
In jedem Satz gibt es einen Fehler. Finde und korrigiere ihn.

1 I didn't play football yesterday because on a school trip I was.

because I was on a school trip

2 My brother a lot of money saved when he wanted to buy a new bike.

3 Helena will become a nurse because always she likes to help people.

4 I'll be home late today because I'll go after school to my friend's house.

5 Samir babysits often his cousin because he gets money for it.

☒ 15 REVISION Jumbled sentences

Write will-future sentences.
Schreibe Sätze im will-future.

1 to our guitar lesson / tomorrow / we / not go

2 you / at the football match / on Saturday / be / ?

3 Peter / his friends / at the youth club / this afternoon / meet

4 become / an architect / one day / I

5 you / do / next weekend / what / ?

6 at school / at 3 o'clock / wait / Mum and Dad / for us

► Check

Hello again! The last day of the holidays

▶ Grammarmaster p. 4

Erklär-film

Revision: Das present progressive

Mit dem *present progressive* sagst du, was jemand jetzt gerade tut. Du beschreibst damit auch, was auf Bildern passiert. Signalwörter für das *present progressive* sind: now (jetzt, gerade), at the moment (im Moment), today (heute).

Das *present progressive* besteht aus zwei Teilen:
be + *verb* + *-ing*
is *watching*

She's looking happy in the photo. (Sie sieht glücklich aus auf dem Foto.)

My parents aren't making lunch today. (Meine Eltern machen heute kein Mittagessen.)

What are you doing at the moment? (Was machst du gerade?)

be
I am / 'm not
he/she/it is / isn't
we/you/they are / aren't

▶ SB p. 173

Unit 1 Travel and holidays

▶ Grammarmaster p. 5

Erklär-film

Das simple past mit *be*

Mit dem *simple past* sprichst du über Dinge, die in der Vergangenheit geschehen sind. Du verwendest es oft mit Zeitangaben wie yesterday (gestern), last week (letzte Woche), in 2022 (2022).

Das Verb *be* hat besondere *simple past*-Formen:

A **bejahte und verneinte Aussagesätze**

I / He / She / It / Noah / Mum	was / wasn't	at home.
You / We / They / My friends	were / weren't	at home.

B **Fragen**

	Was	he / she	at home?
	Were	you / they	at home?
Where	were	you	?

▶ SB p. 13, p. 174

▶ Grammarmaster p. 6

Erklär-film

Das simple past: Bejahte Aussagesätze mit regelmäßigen Verben

Bei regelmäßigen Verben hängst du *-ed* an das Verb an. Es gibt nur eine Form für alle Personen:

I/you/he/she/it/we/you/they talked, looked, watched, ...

Endet das Verb auf *-e*, hängst du nur *-d* an: *dance → danced, like → liked, save → saved*

▶ SB p. 14, p. 174

▸ Grammarmaster pp. 7–8

Das simple past: Bejahte Aussagesätze mit unregelmäßigen Verben

Einige Verben haben unregelmäßige Formen im *simple past*, z. B.:

do	→	did	run	→	ran
go	→	went	see	→	saw
have	→	had	write	→	wrote

Diese Formen musst du lernen.

▸ SB p. 16, p. 174, p. 271

▸ Grammarmaster pp. 9–10

Erklärfilm

Das simple past: Verneinte Aussagesätze

Willst du sagen, dass etwas nicht geschah, stellst du didn't vor die Grundform des Verbs. *Didn't* verwendest du bei allen Personen.

Ben didn't like the food. (Ben mochte das Essen nicht.)

We didn't go out last Friday. (Wir gingen letzten Freitag nicht aus.)

▸ SB p. 20, p. 175

Unit 2 Friends and heroes

▸ Grammarmaster pp. 12–13

Erklärfilm

Das simple past: Fragen und Kurzantworten

Fragen im *simple past* bildest du mit did und der Grundform des Verbs. Auf Entscheidungsfragen antwortest du mit Kurzantworten.

Did Gina visit her friends last week? – Yes, she did. / No, she didn't.
(Hat Gina letzte Woche ihre Freunde besucht? – Ja, hat sie. / Nein, hat sie nicht.)

▸ SB p. 46, p. 175

▸ Grammarmaster p. 14

Erklärfilm

Das simple past: Fragen mit Fragewörtern

Auch Fragen mit Fragewörtern bildest du mit *did*. Das Fragewort steht immer am Satzanfang.

Fragewort	did	Person	Verb im Infinitiv		
Where	*did*	*Lily*	*take*	*the photo?*	*(Wo hat Lily das Foto gemacht?)*
When	*did*	*she*	*take*	*the photo?*	*(Wann hat sie das Foto gemacht?)*

▸ SB p. 47, p. 175

▶ Grammarmaster p. 15

Nebensätze mit Konjunktionen

Konjunktionen verwendest du, um Sätze miteinander zu verknüpfen. Die Wortstellung im Hauptsatz und im Nebensatz ist immer gleich: subject – verb – object.

subject	verb	object	Konjunktion	subject	verb	object
I	*have*	*a snack*	*when*	*I*	*'m*	*hungry.*
They	*got*	*the bus*	*because*	*they*	*didn't want*	*to walk.*

▶ SB p. 68, p. 176

Unit 3 Activities and games

▶ Grammarmaster pp. 17–18

Erklär-film

Das Futur mit going to

Mit *going to* sagst du, dass du etwas in der Zukunft plantst (*after school, tomorrow, next week*).
I'm going to bedeutetet „Ich werde" oder „Ich habe vor".

I'm going to go to a holiday camp this summer. (Ich werde diesen Sommer in ein Ferienlager fahren.)
My parents aren't going to buy a new car this year. (Meine Eltern haben nicht vor, dieses Jahr ein neues Auto zu kaufen.)
Is Holly going to visit her grandma tomorrow? (Wird Holly morgen ihre Großmutter besuchen?)

▶ SB p. 73, pp. 176–177

▶ Grammarmaster pp. 19–20

Erklär-film

Die Steigerung von Adjektiven: Komparativ

Mit den Steigerungsformen der Adjektive kannst du Dinge oder Personen miteinander vergleichen.

A Bei einsilbigen Adjektiven und zweisilbigen Adjektiven, die auf *-y* enden, hängst du *-er* an. Beachte die Schreibweise:

old	*older (than)*	*My mum is older than my dad.*
easy	*easier (than)*	*I think English is easier than French.*
big	*bigger (than)*	*Emre's dog is bigger than Nila's dog.*

B Hat das Adjektiv drei oder mehr Silben oder zwei Silben und endet nicht auf *-y*, steigerst du es mit more.

famous	*more famous (than)*	*Spiderman is more famous than Captain Planet.*
expensive	*more expensive (than)*	*A car is more expensive than a bike.*
interesting	*more interesting (than)*	*This book is more interesting than the others.*

▶ SB p. 77, p. 178

▶ Grammarmaster pp. 21–22

Erklärfilm

Die Steigerung von Adjektiven: Superlativ

Möchtest du sagen, dass etwas am besten, größten, teuersten usw. ist, verwendest du den Superlativ.

A Bei einsilbigen Adjektiven und zweisilbigen Adjektiven, die auf *-y* enden, hängst du *-est* an. Beachte wieder die Schreibweise:

old	*the oldest*	*Dima is the oldest boy in class.*
funny	*the funniest*	*Megastorm is the funniest superhero.*
big	*the biggest*	*We live in the biggest house in the road.*

B Hat das Adjektiv drei oder mehr Silben oder zwei Silben und endet nicht auf *-y*, bildest du den Superlativ mit most.

beautiful	*the most beautiful*	*Roses are the most beautiful flowers.*
important	*the most important*	*This is the most important competition of the year.*

▶ SB p. 78, p. 178

Unit 4 Celebrate!

▶ Grammarmaster pp. 36–37

Erklärfilm

Some / any

Wenn du über eine Menge oder Anzahl sprechen möchtest, du diese Menge oder Anzahl aber nicht genau kennst, verwendest du im Englischen *some* und *any*.

some
- bedeutet „einige", „etwas"
- in bejahten Sätzen
- wenn du um etwas bittest
- wenn du etwas anbietest

Zane invited some friends. (einige Freunde)
Can I have some biscuits, please? (einige Kekse)
Would you like some water? (etwas Wasser)

any
- bedeutet „kein", „keine", „keinen"
- in verneinten Sätzen
- in Fragen

My parents and I don't eat any meat. (kein Fleisch)
Are there any chairs in the classroom? (keine Stühle)

▶ SB p. 101, p. 179

▶ Grammarmaster p. 38

Erklärfilm

A little / a few

Du weißt schon, wie du über große Mengen sprechen kannst. Du verwendest dafür *much* für nicht zählbare Dinge und *many* für zählbare Dinge. Möchtest du aber über kleine Mengen sprechen, verwendest du a little und a few.

a little
- bedeutet „ein wenig", „etwas"
- bei nicht zählbaren Nomen, das heißt, du kannst von diesen Nomen keinen Plural bilden *(water, juice, music, love, money)*

I need a little fruit for my cake. (ein wenig Obst)
Can I have a little sugar for my tea, please? (etwas Zucker)

a few
- bedeutet „einige", „ein paar"
- bei zählbaren Nomen, das heißt, du kannst einen Plural bilden *(one apple, two apples)*

There were a few mistakes in your test. (einige Fehler)
There are only a few strawberries left. (ein paar Erdbeeren)

▶ SB p. 102, p. 179

▸ Grammarmaster p. 39

Zusammensetzungen mit *some* und *any*

- In bejahten Aussagesätzen verwendest du: *somebody/someone, something, somewhere*
  There's somebody in the house. (Da ist jemand im Haus.)
  I can do something nice for my mum. (Ich kann etwas Schönes für meine Mutter machen.)
  My friend is somewhere in the classroom. (Mein Freund ist irgendwo im Klassenraum.)
- In verneinten Aussagesätzen und Fragen verwendest du: *anybody/anyone, anything, anywhere*
  Is there anybody at school today? (Ist heute jemand in der Schule?)
  There isn't anything to eat! (Es gibt nichts zu essen.)
  Can you see my phone anywhere? (Kannst du irgendwo mein Telefon sehen?) ▸ SB p. 109, p. 181

▸ Grammarmaster pp. 40–41

Erklärfilm

Das present perfect

Mit dem *present perfect* sagst du, dass jemand irgendwann etwas getan hat oder dass irgendwann etwas geschehen ist. Der genaue Zeitpunkt des Geschehens ist unwichtig oder unbekannt.

We've played basketball a lot of times. (Wir haben oft Basketball gespielt.)
Mara hasn't visited Brighton. (Mara ist nicht in Brighton gewesen.)
Have you finished your homework? – Yes, I have. (Hast du deine Hausaufgaben gemacht? – Ja, habe ich.)

! Manche Verben haben eine besondere Form.

Ahmet has been to Scotland very often. (Ahmet ist oft in Schottland gewesen.)
My parents haven't had a car yet. (Meine Eltern haben noch kein Auto gehabt.)
Has Louisa met Paolo? – Yes, she has. (Hat Louisa Paolo getroffen? – Ja, hat sie.) ▸ SB p. 105, pp. 180–181, p. 271

Unit 5 Getting ready for the future

▸ Grammarmaster pp. 43–44

Erklärfilm

Das will-future: Bejahte und verneinte Aussagesätze

Du verwendest das *will-future*, wenn du sagen willst, was in der Zukunft wahrscheinlich geschehen wird. Oft verwendest du es mit *I think, maybe, I'm sure*.

A **Bejahte Aussagesätze**

I / you / he / she / it / we / you / they	will / 'll	+ Grundform des Verbs	*I think we'll stay at home tomorrow. It'll be rainy. (Ich denke, wir werden morgen zu Hause bleiben. Es wird regnerisch.)*

B **Verneinte Aussagesätze**

I / you / he / she / it / we / you / they	will not / won't	+ Grundform des Verbs	*I'm sure I won't become a programmer. (Ich bin sicher, dass ich kein Programmierer werde.)*

▸ SB p. 132, p. 182

▸ Grammarmaster pp. 45–46

Erklär-film

Das will-future: Fragen und Kurzantworten

Bei Fragen im *will-future* steht *will* am Satzanfang. Hat die Frage ein Fragewort, steht das noch davor.

	Will your sister be at the party? – Yes, she will. (Wird deine Schwester auf der Party sein? – Ja, wird sie.)
	Will you meet Oscar tomorrow? – No, I won't. (Wirst du Oscar morgen treffen? – Nein, werde ich nicht.)
When	*will she arrive? – At 8 o'clock. (Wann wird sie ankommen? – Um 8 Uhr.)*
Where	*will we meet? – In front of the cinema. (Wo werden wir uns treffen? – Vor dem Kino.)*

▸ SB p. 132, p. 182

▸ Grammarmaster pp. 47–48

Die Wortstellung

Im englischen Aussagesatz ist die Wortstellung immer subject – verb – object:

I meet my friends when we play football together.

Eine Ortsangabe steht meist nach Verb und Objekt.

Subjekt	Verb	Objekt	Ort
I	*meet*	*my friends*	*at school.*

Zeitangaben stehen am Anfang oder am Ende des Satzes.

Zeit	Subjekt	Verb	Objekt	Zeit
Every day	*I*	*meet*	*my friends.*	
	I	*meet*	*my friends*	*every day.*

▸ SB p. 137, p. 182